The Little Frog

By Crista Stewart

Illustrated by Sarah Cressler

Halo ●●●●
Publishing International

The Little Frog
First Edition February 2009
Text Copyright © 2009 Crista Stewart
Library of Congress Control Number: 2008942940
ISBN 13: 978-0-9797429-9-6

Please Visit Crista Stewart At:
www.halopublishing.com
or
www.cristastewartslittlefrog.com

Published by

Publishing International
www.halopublishing.com
Telephone (216) 255-6756

Printed in the United States of America

To my Crista's Loving
husband, Eric. Her
adoring little frogs,
Makenzie, Irelynd,
Haley, and Gage. Also,
her supportive parents,
Clyde and Carol and
most importantly, God.
She loves you
all so much!
Thanks,

Little Frog

One day in September, something special happened…

A frog was born by a pond in a town called Mudville.

The frog's name was Little Frog.

Little Frog was different from all the other Mudville frogs.

He was much smaller. His green skin was not a beautiful shade of green like all the others.

And… Little Frog only had three legs.

Most days, Little Frog would sit by his little rock.

He would spend lots of time watching the big beautiful green frogs play and jump around on their four legs.

The big frogs did not invite Little Frog to play in their games.

There were many times when the big frogs would tease Little Frog.

One day, Little Frog overheard one of the big beautiful green frogs say, "Little Frog is so small. He hops so slowly."

Little Frog wished he had a friend who liked him just the way he was.

Every night, while all the other frogs were asleep, Little Frog would stay awake and look up at the night sky.

Little Frog never took the time to pray because he did not think God liked him.

But one night, Little Frog did something different.

Little Frog prayed, "Hello God, do you know me?"

God answered, "Hello, dear Little Frog. I am so glad you called to me. I have been waiting to hear from you."

Little Frog could not believe God was waiting to hear from him.

After a moment, Little Frog asked, "Well… why did you make me this way? I am so different. Do you not like me?"

God answered, "Oh, Little Frog, I love you. Someday you will understand. Rely on me, I am your friend."

Little Frog dozed off to sleep with a smile.

He felt very happy inside.

Little Frog began to talk with God every day.

Soon, he did not care if the big beautiful green frogs did not invite him to play their games. He had a friend he could rely on.

God liked Little Frog just the way he was.

One day, Little Frog decided to venture away from his little rock.

He slowly hopped to the other side of the pond.

Little Frog could not believe the beautiful scenery.

He saw colorful flowers, tall green grass, and a bright red bench.

Little Frog was tired from hopping, so he decided to rest under the bright red bench.

The cool shade felt good to Little Frog.

He closed his eyes and took a nap.

Little Frog suddenly awoke with a jump!

He was surprised to see two big blue eyes staring back at him.

Little Frog started to hop away, but the boy with the big blue eyes scooped Little Frog into his hand.

"Look, Mom, the Little Frog is missing his leg. He looks like me!"

Little Frog looked up at the boy with blue eyes, fire-engine red hair, and freckles.

Then Little Frog looked down and noticed the boy had only one arm.

Little Frog thought, "*I found someone who will understand exactly how I feel.*"

This made Little Frog very happy.

The boy, Chase, made a nice home for Little Frog by the pond in his backyard.

Little Frog and Chase spent lots of time together talking and playing.

Chase did not have many friends in his neighborhood because the other children did not know how to react to Chase's missing arm.

But they heard about Little Frog and wanted to meet him.

Little Frog and Chase had a wonderful day playing with their new friends.

At the end of the day, Chase said goodbye to his new friends.

He gave Little Frog a good night kiss and walked back to his house.

Little Frog looked up at the night sky and prayed...

"Thank you for helping me rely on you.
Now I understand why you made me the way you did.
You wanted me to help others who are different like me.
You are such an awesome God!
Amen!"

Parent Resource Guide

FROG stands for Fully Rely On God

Little Frog

Activity:

Take your child/children outside to look for a very special rock.
Use a permanent marker to write *Isaiah 26:4*.
Refer to *Isaiah 26:4* in the Bible.
Isaiah 26:4 "Trust in the Lord forever for the Lord God is an everlasting rock."

Prayer:

Dear God,

Please help me to learn, like Little Frog, how to rely on you completely.
Please be my everlasting rock.
In Jesus name, I pray.

Amen

Amazing Facts about Frogs

Did you know the world's largest frog is called the Goliath frog?
You can find it in moving rivers and streams with sandy bottoms in West Africa.
Did you know the smallest frog is called the Gold frog?
You can find it in the Southern Hemisphere, mainly in Brazil.

The Lifecycle of a frog is called
METAMORPHOSIS (meta-mor-pho-sis)

Metamorphosis means the change of shape during an animal's life. Life as
a Christian is like a metamorphosis. Our heart, our choices, and our life go
through a metamorphosis or change when we fully rely on God.

My Prayers …

Little Frog

Kid's Page

We are all different in some way. Is there anything about you that is different? If yes, write about what is different about you?

_____

_____

_____

_____

_____

_____

Are you like Little Frog, and wonder why God made you the way you are? If yes, please remember that God made you the way you are for a reason. Trust in God, and know that He made you for a purpose.

Write or draw a picture about a time when you Fully Relied On God
(FROG)

Printed in the United States
154481LV00001B